Map of Northern California, indicating Hoopa Valley
Rand McNally & Co, Chicago, IL, 1956.

THE WHITE-SKIN DEER:

Hoopa Stories

by

ELIZABETH SCHULTZ

Mammoth Publications
Lawrence, Kansas

Mammoth Publications
1916 Stratford Rd.
Lawrence, Kansas 66044-4540

Contact : mammothpubs@hotmail.com
Order: www.mammothpublications.com

Published by Mammoth Publications
Typesetting by Pamela LeRow
Book design by Denise Low
Printed by Lightning Source
Cover design by Pamela LeRow
Cover photograph by Marilyn Tucker

ISBN   0-9800102-2-5
ISBN   978-0-9800102-2-0

ACKNOWLEDGEMENTS

Both "The River" and "The Brush-Dance" (formerly "The Chief") were previously published in issues of the Wellesley College literary journal, *Keynote*, 1957-58. "Bone" first appeared in *Cimarron Review* in 1971 and was reprinted in *Images of Women in Literature*, edited by Mary Anne Ferguson (3rd. edition, Houghton Mifflin 1981). "The White-Skin Deer" was published as "The Last of the White-Skin Deer" in *Kansas Quarterly* in 1975.

That this collection of stories has a new life in print is due to Pam LeRow of University of Kansas' College of Liberal Arts & Sciences Digital Media Services, whose care and help have been so generous, and to Denise Low-Weso, whose friendship and wisdom have been lodestars for many years. I am also thankful to Tami Albin for her patient help with photographic reproduction on a rainy day.

Donald Davis, American Friends Service Committee Archivist in Philadelphia, was also very helpful in tracking down material about the 1956 Hoopa Valley workcamp. I am especially filled with gratitude to Sherrie, Marilyn, and Roy Tucker as well as the Friends of the Redwood Libraries, the Humboldt County Historical Society, and the Hoopa Library, all of whom have helped to make it possible for me to connect again not only with a critical part of my past but also with their ongoing and vital community and with a place filled with history and beauty. My thanks ongoing to the ancestors.

CONTENTS

ACKNOWLEDGEMENTS   iii

INTRODUCTION   vii

PREFACE   ix

THE RIVER   1

THE BRUSH-DANCE   11

BONE   21

THE WHITE-SKIN DEER   31

HOOPA VALLEY PORTFOLIO   51

BIOGRAPHY   59

INTRODUCTION

Mammoth Publications presents history, books, and electronic media that otherwise would not be available to the public. Some of our books include Theresa Milk's history of Haskell Institute, an early American Indian boarding school; Ojibwa poet E. Donald Two-Rivers' *Powwows, Fat Cats, and Other Indian Tales*; and a documentary history of Langston Hughes's boyhood in Lawrence, Kansas.

The White-Skin Deer: Hoopa Stories follows the Mammoth mission of recovering histories. It is a first-hand, fictionalized account of tribal elders' stories, written by a sincere and respectful non-Native woman, Elizabeth Schultz. Schultz wrote these stories based on her experiences living on the Hoopa Valley Tribe's land during the 1950s. This was a time period when Bureau of Indian Affairs policies of assimilation were at their height. Their boarding elementary and high schools actively worked against Native cultural practices, including Native language, ceremonies, economic systems, and kinship responsibilities.

Like all good fiction, these stories prompt reflection. Embedded within them are the conflicts facing most American tribal peoples at that time. A young man is torn between employment hours at the sawmill and the Hoopa ceremonial calendar. He also is torn between respecting his family's dance objects and the temptation of selling them to collectors. In the story "The River," an elder survives a springtime flood but loses community spiritual protection when church people violate a Hoopa burial ground. In "The Brush-Dance," another elder suffers the effects of alcohol, but he nonetheless transmits the essential ceremonial dance to the next generation. The issues confronted by the fictional and non-fictional characters in these stories are continuing challenges for all American communities.

Within each story is a triumph: survivance, to use Ojibwa writer Gerald Vizenor's term that means more than basic survival. In the story "Bone," an elder proves to have a cache of personal and sacred objects hidden away. These objects are like the orally transmitted knowledge that also was kept private. Thus it continues to be renewed. Hoopa people still live in the Trinity River Valley on their land and flourish.

Elizabeth Schultz, friend and mentor for forty years, must have been a remarkable young woman. While still a college student, the elders must have noticed her reflective, articulate nature, because they told her, an outsider, some of their privileged oral tradition. Schultz responded with the most respectful gratitude she knew, saving these stories in literary form.

These stories are framed in the European-American short story idiom of the English language, yet they relay observations of importance to all peoples. Schultz's rich style, full of details about people and the land, is already mature. She appropriately places each story within the context of river and mountains. She leaves parts of the stories untold, so readers may participate in their dynamism.

Her gift is to return these stories, after more than fifty years, to the Hoopa people, first, and other readers who may not otherwise know about the strong Hoopa elders who preserved their traditional ways despite many struggles. Mammoth Publications is honored to be part of this circle.

Thomas Pecore Weso, Menominee Nation
Denise Low
2009

PREFACE

Thinking back to my 1956 summer in the Hoopa Valley Tribal Reservation, I remember first the air: hot and dry, but always light. Here in a deep river valley in northern California's Sierra Madres, each year the Hoopa people perform rituals to renew the world—to keep the air light, to keep the rivers clean, and to keep the salmon and the acorns, their traditional foods, plentiful. As a participant in an American Friends Service Committee work camp, I had come to Hoopa Valley with a group of sixteen college students from the United States and Europe. Arriving on July Fourth, our introduction to Hoopa was three days of celebration—not only a patriotic parade and pageant around the reservation center with tribal members and local non-Hoopa people participating, but also Hoopa races, stick games, and a dance where tribal members drummed and conducted a healing ceremony.

As a result of severe flooding in the valley that spring, we were assigned a diversity of tasks. Most meaningful were those tasks which allowed us to work alongside Hoopa people in rebuilding their homes. Although some Hoopas who lived in traditional cedar plank buildings on high ground in mountain meadows had not been affected by the flood, we helped others whose homes were closer to the river to shovel out mud, re-set fence posts, wash cupboards, lay new flooring, put up sheetrock, and paint. No girls were permitted to assist with removing mud from the sacred Gods' House. All of us, however, worked clearing brush to save the madrone trees on a site for a new hospital as well as organizing Saturday night square dances and a community theater production, which turned out to be *Oklahoma*. In the late afternoon, we cooled off by swimming in the rushing waters of Campbell Creek and Trinity River.

There were also days when time opened up for us and deepened across the valley, into the forests, following the river's meandering course, into the clouds gathering on the mountains. These were times when Hoopa people invited us to join them in gathering wild berries, apples, herbs, and flowers; in watching pottery being made and painted with the geometrical Hoopa designs that also appear in their basketry; in sharing a meal of smoked salmon, venison, home-made bread with home-made plum jam, and stupendous cakes and pies; and in sitting quietly on a porch or on blankets laid out in a meadow as shadows flowed across the mountains. These were times spent with Hoopa people breathing the light air together.

The first two stories in the collection presented here were written following my return to college, and the following two were written some years later. In reviving these stories now, so many years after they were written, I am humbled by my audacity in attempting to portray the dignity and integrity of the Hoopa people I met more than fifty years ago. I can only hope to thank their descendants now and to thank the old ones in memory for showing me a way to be in the world, in particular for guiding me toward an understanding of the profound connections between a people and a place.

Elizabeth Schultz
2009

THE RIVER

In the valley there was never a spring time, and there was never a fall time. There was no special time for things to grow from the ground gradually; there was no special time for things to turn back into the ground. Only suddenly were there strong green stalks. There was no spreading of summer into winter. The change happened sharply.

With the river, the change also happened that way. It moved in accordance with the winter and the summer.

The beginning of the river was high. In the earliest time, the old people of the valley said it had a spirit source. They came to know its origin in the Upper Klamath Lake and its clear silences. They came to know how it went the many miles slantwise, slashing out the gorges and ripping raggedly around the rocks, finally rolling out into the valley between the dipping trees. And they came to know that when the summer stopped, and suddenly it was winter with the snows in the mountains and the rushing rains in the valley, the river became mighty.

That last winter was the worst. The river swelled with the snows until it surged over its sides and submerged the low center of the valley and its trees. It swirled chickens and coops up into its midstream and wheelbarrows and boxes and bed springs. It smashed down the sawdust burners by the mill and swept through the bridge. It entered windows and cupboards. Loretta Jesse, who was old, said it must have been some evil in the valley that made the bad spirit in the river rage so. It took away the Gods' House, which was made in the first time by the old people. It was made with red cedar brought down from the far forest. The old people called the house long-lasting like the spirits and the gods. In the rich red wood there had never been any worm-holes. Loretta Jesse said later that during this time, when the river was the worst, she saw a horse white like fresh

1

mist moving. He was on a piece of top-ground, and the river all around it churned in circles, and he cried high in the wind.

It was Loretta who remembered about Wilma Melton and told somebody to take a boat across the river to see how things were with her. Wilma Melton lived by the brush-dance pit, over by the Gods' House.

So two boys went in a boat across the river and the low part of the valley among the tops of the trees, to the place where they had the brush-dance. The river had fallen down into the pit and filled it to be even with itself. Only the ring of seats around the pit, rising out of the river as a reef, showed the boys the place of the pit. Beyond was Wilma Melton's house. The river was just reaching up to it. It had squeezed through the grasses and was making sporadic swishes at the edge of the house. It had moved through the fence that squared off Wilma Melton's cemetery, where the old fathers were kept. Through the fence it had twisted scraggy roots and branches.

The river had struck the out shed and shifted it strangely, but Wilma Melton's house had stuck to the ground. It was made from skinny boards and seemed small against the river-rising. Its brownness was folded into the vast void of grey wind and rain. At first, to the boys in the boat, it seemed to be floating in the grayness. Then the river heaped them up solid on the shore around the house. They dumped themselves out. The oldest one took the line strung through the boat's nose and brought the boat up on the mucky land near the house. The other one pounded on the door. The sound was blown away so that between the boys, there was only the noise of the rain. The hollowness from inside the house scooped out a small hollow feeling in their own stomachs. Again, the one pounded out on the door and the other made the words, "Wilma Melton," close to the door hinge so the sound would go inside.

From the space in the house somebody said something in old Hoopa, and then, "What you ghost guys want in here?"

The biggest boy spoke again, "Wilma Melton, we come to help. We come from Loretta Jesse. Across the river way."

And the other boy spoke now, "We come to get you. If you'll come." All around was the rain thudding down into the ground.

"Who is that there?" somebody said from the inside of the house.

One boy answered, "We come from Loretta Jesse. We are Hank Henderson and Dale Kindness. We come to see if you are all right because the river is getting very bad. Sure. Can we come into this house?" In a flick of the wind, a wooden trapeze for summer roses was splintered and sent off from the house. The boys opened the door.

The hollow house sucked in the wind. The boys had to crease the door back. Wilma Melton was sitting close under the roof on a rafter. The house contained the cold and the wind distilled. Outside, the great mass of wind was moving past, skittering the sticks and the splintered rose trapeze; inside, the cold air was immobile. In a corner of the house were kept the grasses gathered from the special places in the mountains for the baskets. Because of the dampness rising off the ground, the grasses smelled ages old. On the walls were the bright pink and blue pictures of white men doing nice things which the church people had sent. There were the Good Samaritan and the man from Jerusalem and the words in wrought Gothic saying, "He had compassion and went to him and bound up his wounds, pouring oil and wine." The floor boards in the house were softened by the padding feet of many years. In the house there were also crates from the San Fernando fruit farms and cans and canning jars with the thick blue glass, also an iron bed and an iron stove. It was by standing on a crate put on top of the stove that Wilma Melton had gotten up to the rafter.

The older boy spoke, "Wilma Melton, are you all right now? We was wondering, we got the boat . . . we better go quick before the river rises up too much more. Loretta Jesse sent us out."

"You get over there," said Wilma Melton from the rafter, "by that bed. I look at you good. To see if you got real teeth."

Again, the older boy spoke, "You got anything like old porcupine hats or stuff that oughta better go out with us?" He was standing stiff with his arms straight down.

"I see now you are Hank Henderson and Dale Kindness. I know your old fathers and old Horsemeat Henderson. And the cousin, but he is no good. You are not the spirits. I prayed to Jesus for somebody come. I been with the spirits a long time now. Maybe I begin to get scared of that spirit in the river. They say in the church-people's book you get scared, you pray to Jesus and things get to be all right." Wilma Melton shoved herself slowly down from the rafter to the crate to the stove. She stood on the front burner and listened with her silence to the shifting sounds outside the house.

Wilma Melton was a small shape. Her basket cap, woven from bark browns and black, grasses, and yellow porcupine quills into patterns of parallelograms, gave form to Wilma Melton. She wore it so close down on her forehead that some long lines of hair were forced from the braid wrapped behind her head. Until she said something to them again, the boys could only stand there. Beyond the house was the sound of the wind washing across the river. Wilma Melton stooped some to stare the boys out of the shadows.

"You have good teeth," was what she said at last. "I pray to Jesus He save me. So I is saved. I pray to Jesus He save my house now."

The other boy stepped out. "Wilma Melton," he said, "we must better be going on."

4

Wilma Melton put on a pink sweater twice-shrunk so that it was a child's size, so the buttons stretched from the button holes. She patted down the bed, pressed out a long wrinkle in the top cover with her thumb, plumped the pillow, and nipped the edges of the covers in all around.

"Hey," said the older boy, "let's move it." Wilma Melton had one more thing to do. She reached into the side of her dress for something.

"Wild celery root," she said. Since the first time, men who carried a dead friend to his place with the fathers sat for a day in the smoke from wild celery root, so that evil spirits from the dead would not stay by them. Wilma Melton lit the piece of wild celery root, worn down to white by rubbing in her pocket. It burned a hole in the darkness, and the smell was acrid. It stabbed the darkness. In a second it glowed out.

One of the boys said, "It's really cold out there." He took the manufactured blanket marked with orange triangles and green zigzags. Wilma Melton shrugged it around her, and they went from the house into the outside.

There was the boat and the wind rushing the river. Wilma Melton pulled the blanket into herself. She spoke to the storm, "You evil spirit that comes in the wind and the water, you go. I had enough. Now I pray to Jesus." And she spoke soft to herself, "I know this Jesus He can save me. Loretta, too, she help send Him."

The boys brought her across the water to Loretta's.

Afterwards everybody knew how bad the river had been in the valley. They knew that it had twisted out the bridge, and the S. A. Nurmi Company from Los Angles had got the contract with the government to raise a temporary one for now and a new steel one by October 15; that it had swept the Trinity Lumber Company's private plane up into a tree; that it had banked houses with mud so that the government had to give out trailers and 87 people had to move to the school cafeteria;

5

that it had drowned three children, a mother, and some others plus chickens, pigs, one horse, geese, porcupines, and a goat. They had seen the pictures. The Red Cross people had come in. They wore visor caps and brought in boxes of food. The government people had come in. They asked many questions, and sometimes they got answers to write down in the long blanks on their sheets. The church people came in when summer was starting. They would help with the houses.

The river, by summer, had seeped back. Over the soft shore and onto the land it had rolled rocks and rocks. They were harsh-cut, up from the bottom, and only the river could roll them back. Beyond the rocks, the river had laid down a massive mud. It was heavy on the bean fields.

Down by Wilma Melton's, the summer river now slid through a wrenched section of the bridge. In the summer it ran slippery-smooth in the valley. It slurred around stones and sent tails sweeping out from behind them. Even at the bottom of the big Blue Slide, where beneath the gliding surface the water was stilled in a milk-green fog and where the old people said there was a way to the cool center of the earth, the river went easily. Later in the summer the salmon would come circling and circling against the current. Until they were swapped up by the men down the river onto the shore and their big silver bodies had started to tarnish, they seemed to be gliding ghosts. In the valley only the Indians could hunt the salmon.

When the winter stopped, Wilma Melton went back to her house. The house had stayed and the out shed, but the stacks of split sugar-pine and the 35 small chicks had been scuttered away. A new dog had come from somewhere. Wilma Melton called him "Smoke." The cemetery was safe because the fence was still strong around it. It was fringed in places with loose lines of grey grass. Sticks crossed through the wires. The church people said they were coming to repair it.

On a morning they drove up to the house in a red-and-black truck with windshield wipers that swiped down from the top. Wilma Melton had brought the iron bed out from the house under the cherry-plum tree where she brought it every summer time. She was sitting small on the mattress so that the sides slanted in to her. By the door into the house was a short wooden stand for some wash things: an enamel pan and soap and two smooth scrubbing stones. Above was hooked an abalone shell of pink and ocean blues and green deepening through each other to a dark rim. Around the house there were berry bushes heaped over with their fruit. A wave of wind came cooling from the river and passed into the cherry-plum tree. There was a sense that everything was perfectly placed in a pattern.

The church people slammed themselves out of the truck and scurried up the soft dust left from the river mud. They were three men and two women. "We're come from the Mission House. We heard you might be needing our help," the biggest man announced and put on a smile. The dog Smoke was whiffing the heels of the man's shoes. The man kicked him off to the side. Smoke shivered up his upper lip.

Wilma Melton said, "He's all right, that dog. Don't worry yourselfs."

"We come," said the second man, "in the name of Jesus Christ to preach good words and to do good works. Have you got any wood to be split, cupboards to be cleaned, cellars to be dug, walls to be washed, sheds to be made, lawns to be raked, fences to be pulled, floors to be laid? We can do it."

"Mrs. Melton . . . I understand that's your name," said the tall woman, "we're just going to sit here under this tree and talk about things. We'll just let those men take care of the work. They're big and can do almost anything." The five church people kept standing in a line.

The woman from the middle spoke, "We will tell you about the Gospels." The wind passed out of the cherry-plum tree with a quiet sound. The little leaves lifted and fell.

The second man spoke again, "I see that fence can use a little repairing. We'll pull out those posts, get you some new posts, tack on a little wire. Just got some new stainless steel kind over at Jordan's Store. Fix you up real fine."

Wilma Melton said, "The fence is good." As long as there was no break in the fence, the spirits of the old fathers were kept inside. "But it could be better," said the big man.

The third man strode over to the fence and shook the first post in its hole until the dust puffed up. "Loose," he said. "Get the pinchers." The men set to clattering the shovels and the other tools inside the truck. The steely sounds crossed sharply against each other and across the softness of the morning. The women sat down by Wilma Melton. They shifted themselves about on the mattress, and by mincing their feet on the ground, they tried to keep from sloping down into her.

"Those guys," Wilma Melton said, "I don't want them doing that thing."

The tall woman explained, "They will make it better. They work for Jesus." Across the river buzzards floated flatly among their own shadows.

Wilma Melton said, "I know this man Jesus. It was many years some other ladies come to me. They had pictures and told me stories about this nice man. Then I get sick with the spirits in me. All night long these ladies come to sit with me and pray to Jesus, oh, Jesus. They don't give me any acorn soup, but I is get some. Pretty soon in many more weeks the burning goes out, and the ladies say it is because of Jesus. I remember this Jesus because they say you pray to Him and you get saved."

The sun had become a great golden globe in the high-sky. The shine coming down from it could not lie glowing heavily on the river as it did on the land. It stippled the river with sparks. "But these guys here," Wilma Melton continued, "should not be going in the place of the fathers. Evil spirits will come out. You see."

The middle lady shook a handkerchief out of her sleeve to dab away the sweaty streaks beside her nose. She asked Wilma Melton a question, "Mrs. Melton, you believe in spirits, don't you? That is a sin. Jesus does not approve of sin." The sun came only in quick flickers under the cherry-plum tree. Wilma Melton split off some shafts of yellow green grass from close by. She drew each piece out through her bottom teeth. She began to fold them tightly over and over each other.

The men pulled through the snags of roots and grass that had been meshed into the fence; they pinched off the fence nails at the corners; they pushed on the posts. "This fence will be the best in all your valley. Better than anybody ever knew!" the big man called out to Wilma Melton.

Overhead, the sun bulged huge. The men knotted the corners of their handkerchiefs and fitted them down on their heads. The big man let the sweat grease down his face. The young man hung his arms down from working and let his hands dangle in the heat. He held his arms off from his body so coolness could come across under the armpits. The heat was heavy yellow. Wilma Melton did not answer.

The middle woman kept talking to her about the rightness and the wrongness. She said that the river rose up because of the wrath of the One God at the people. She took out a Bible from her bosom and read from Genesis, "'Now the earth was corrupt in God's sight, and the earth was filled with violence . . . Then the Lord said to Noah . . . in seven days I will send rain upon the earth for forty days and forty nights, and every living thing that I have made, I will blot out from the face of the earth.' Your Gods' House is gone now."

9

The men from under the cherry-plum tree seemed to move through the heat like ten-thumbed giants. The second one was heaving the fence posts back and forth. The sweat glossed over his forehead and was coming into the corners of his eyes. He made a final heave and fell over fainting. The other men came to him first. The young man called out, "Bob, Bob, what's the matter, anyways?" and then the women got up from the mattress to see. It slanted back down again to Wilma Melton.

"Oh," said the tall woman, "something has happened. Good heavens, we better go help." The two women went to help with carrying their man back into the truck. Wilma Melton was sitting still under the cherry-plum tree when they all went off in the red-and-black truck. The dried river dust settled back into its softness.

Wilma Melton answered, "The Gods' House now gone. The fence is not now good with those holes. And the old fathers are moving around."

In the evening the shadows floated into the valley, and Wilma Melton told Smoke to get gone to the house. Under the cherry-plum tree, she fixed herself for sleeping. The coolness of the clean night came, and she fell to listening to the small sounds of the grass insects and the summer stirrings of the river, never still.

THE BRUSH-DANCE

Over on the other side of the river was the Square. It was along the road to Willow Creek, almost outside the valley. The Square people always said that Ulysses S. Grant had his headquarters in the stucco house on the west side when he was in California with the army fighting the Hoopa people. If anyone came to the Square, they always pointed the house out. There were other houses on the Square, but they were mostly shingle and were small except for the two that had summer porches where people could sit at night after the dust from the day had sifted down, listening to the sprinklers chinking. On the other sides of the Square were the offices of the Bureau of Indian Affairs and the trailers for the Forestry Service and the old government school where they had first made the Hoopa children come. A tennis court of coarse sand cement, cracked and overrun with stubble, was in the center of the Square. In December there had been a flood in the valley, but it hadn't reached up to the Square.

The Fourth of July was the biggest thing that happened in the Square. In the old time, the Hoopas used to have a Sun Day Ceremony in the first part of this month. All that was left of it was the brush-dance, which still had to be in the pit. There could only be one pit. There could only be one Gods' House, too, except now the Gods' House was gone because the flood had come up. And now even the brush-dance happened on the Fourth of July.

The parade around the Square began at 11:00 A.M. There were red-white-and-blue crepe-paper strips hanging off the side of the school, twisted up the tree trunks, tied on the tree twigs. There were green ash trees on the edge of the Square. Their leaves were finely feathered, and with any wind they

11

fluttered against each other while the red-white-and-blue strips tied on the twigs floated out over the Square.

Besides people from the Square, others had come from Willow Creek and Humboldt. They were standing all around and sweating in their summer cottons. Someone said there were going to be Hoopa people in the parade. Mr. Frank Gordon, who was with the Bureau, was starting to speak up on the steps of the school. He said, "The Indians of this valley are a proud people . . . together we are a proud nation . . . ever since that proud day when the Founding Fathers sat down at a table in the city of Philadelphia and wrote out and signed that proud document, the Declaration of Independence . . . together let us say, 'One nation, indivisible, with liberty and justice for all' . . . and so help us, may we all have a snorting good time today here in the valley."

The motion was seconded, and Mr. Frank Gordon spoke again, "Send out the band boys, and a gold statuette for the most original float, the best Indian float, the float with the prettiest girls, the most interesting float sponsored by a commercial corporation. All for the people . . ."

The parade started with many bicycles. They had red-white-and-blue strips wrapped around the handle-bars and woven into the wheels. The boys in the pink-gold-and-turquoise striped T-shirts rode them in and out of the parade, around and around the Square, and the wheels whirred, blurring the red-white-and-blue. They rode them in between the Jordan Store float with its display of Big Badger power saws and the Community Hospital fund float and the Hoopa float that some of the mothers had got up for old times' sake. It had fir branches fastened on the four corners, and the Marshall twins and the Hailstone boys stood up there with their shirts off. They carried a couple of quivers. Sitting on the hospital float bed was Rachel Parker, who still had the long blue tattoo lines left from the old times streaking her chin. She sat there and kept pulling a slow smile across her gums. Everybody loved Rachel Parker and brought her magazines with pictures and gave her birthday parties. In the parade there were also horses that reared on their back legs before all the people and the troop of Cub Scouts that stepped together, not-together. In and out, the bicycles went with their churning colors.

Most of the grown-ups stayed in front of the school so they could clap whenever something went by Mr. Frank Gordon, but the children scattered across the stubble-weed in the center of the Square with their dogs circling around them. Some of them got nickels and bought red candy apples.

Ray Fischer wanted to give one of them a nickel, but he couldn't. They all ran off sideways to watch the parade some more when he came up. Ray Fischer had been drunk since about 5:30 yesterday afternoon. He sat on a box under one of the trees where the shade was a warm softness when the parade started. Except by the trees, there was no shade in the Square. The sun had focused down into it, making everything sharply bright. Now Ray Fischer went over to the people. He had a strength in his legs even though his shoulders were sloped down so that his arms were long. In his face, his eyes were rusty-red, lost in his wrinkles. Even in the sun, Ray Fischer wore a sheep skin, tanned and turned so the wooly bulk was inside.

Some of the people who weren't exactly watching the parade saw him coming and shifted away. They thought most Hoopas went up in the hills, at least until the brush-dance, which didn't start up until around 8:00. Ray Fischer wanted to speak to the people. He went first to one lady. "Ain't it pretty like?" he asked. He said things slowly, but there was a high sound stitched into his speech.

The lady shrugged herself, "I'm sure it's very nice."

"You are pretty-lady," Ray Fischer smiled with his mouth

open, showing his tongue.

The lady said, "Thanks, I'm sure."

A friend who was with her said, "So long, Bonzo." They stepped away. The parade had passed all around the Square now, and Mr. Frank Gordon was giving out the gold statuettes. People were beginning to press into their own groups. Ray Fischer poked out one finger to touch another lady. "Ain't it pretty like?" he asked again.

She pivoted. "Merciful heavens, you give a person a fright. What do you mean? That little gold prize? I should say it is lovely, but that don't mean I'd want it sitting in my living room. Say . . ." and she looked at Ray Fischer straight. He was touching the tip of his tongue to his top lip. "Aren't you old Ray Fischer? Aren't you one of the chiefs of the old tribe? I've heard some stories about you."

"You are pretty-lady, nice," said Ray Fischer.

She went on. "You going to be leading off over at the brush-dance tonight. We came from out past Willa Creek to see it."

"You come for brush-dance? I like you-lady, pretty-lady. I be going in brush-dance."

"Yes," the lady said, "we're coming round to the brush-day. That'll be real nice."

Ray Fischer was squeezing and squeezing his hands over his thumbs and then his hands together, and then he reached out and squeezed the lady's hands into his. "I show brush-dance now," he said. "I chief." The whole wide sky had become concentrated in the sun. Its heat had drawn off all colors so that everything in the Square was dulled down. People's outlines had disappeared because of the dustiness of the Square. Everybody was mussed.

There were some men standing around on the Square and watching things. Two flexed forward. "Hey you," one spoke to Ray Fischer, "leave the lady alone."

The other added, "Lady, that Indian is as drunk as a loon."

She said, "Yes, he is. He was trying to hold my hand."

The man set his hands on Ray Fischer's shoulders and said, "Scram outa here or get sober. This is a decent show."

"You come brush-dance? I show," said Ray Fischer. The men shoved him away.

"Okay, we'll have our eyes out for you anyways," the lady responded. She was shaking her hands out by her sides so the wetness from Ray's squeezing would dry off in the dust.

He turned out of the Square and took the road down to the river. The heat hung heavy and the thick thrumming of insects had settled into it. Along the road there were stiff thistles growing up from the low grass. In this heat the grass and thistles were the color of dust. Ray Fischer shuffled up the little road rocks. His head seemed small, as if separated from the sheep skin coat. He crossed the cow-catch carefully, setting down each foot straight along the diagonal, so he would not sink into it.

He crossed the river the same way. The bridge was down by Blue Slide, so he had to use the stones. Because the bank was soft, steep sand, he only took a beginning step and then let himself slide down to the bottom where the sand had a hard, smooth edge. The top bank sand was sun-scorched and made a searing streak beneath him when he was coming down, but at the bottom it was cool. The river rustled against it, and Ray Fischer rested before he made the crossing. His old father knew how to run the river in a canoe and had showed him how to step across it even where it had turned into a whirling whiteness.

Out from the shore the river was rapid. It spun spirals around the stones and spun spray into the air. Ray Fischer set out his foot carefully on a stone. There was water whisking all round him and nothing solid except the single stone. He stepped straight.

When he was on the other side, he went over to the Jordan Store so he could sit around out back in the sawdust where they kept the great glassy chunks of ice. He wanted to stay cool. Some of the big pudgy boys were already there with beer. They were squirting each other with Dial deodorant in the orange squeeze bottle when he came up. Their skin was sticky. "Old Ray," they said, "how's it gonna be up at the dance tonight? Are you gonna show us how to sing?"

Ray Fischer said, "I show you. I old man chief. I show you young boys. I show you."

"We'll really show 'em, won't we?" they said. "Love to dance the cha-cha," they said, lilting the words.

Ray Fischer said, "I do brush-dance."

"Sure you do brush-dance. We do brush-dance, cha-cha, cha-cha, cha-cha," and they rolled in the sawdust. "Show us, Pops!"

"You no-good Indian boys," said Ray Fischer.

One of them said, "Show us like up at the old Gods' House."

Ray Fischer put one hand half around his mouth and began a hollow humming. The high sound was still in his voice. "That's hot, cha-cha," they all said. "Have a beer. It's Jordan's best." They butted in a beer can and gave it to him with the foam floating around its rim.

"Old Hardrock bringing the dance feathers tonight? He gonna be there?" they asked.

"Old Hardrock, he don't drink none, does he? Not like old Ray," they said.

"Show you dance" said Ray Fischer.

"Have some beer," they offered. "Beer good." And they fixed another can and another can.

"Show dance now," said Ray Fischer, and he sat down in the damp brown sawdust. The sheep skin sagged. "Beer bad. Give me 'nother beer," he demanded.

The boys burrowed into the sawdust until they came up with five more packs. They kept giving him beer until it was leaking out of his mouth onto the sheep skin into the sawdust. They asked Ray Fischer, "How many babes are gonna be in the dance tonight?"

One of them had a tattoo inscribed on his arm. "That's my Indian princess," he said, and he rocked his arm.

"We wanna know about the babes, Pops," they said, but Ray Fischer didn't know any more. They left him then.

Ray Fischer stayed in the sawdust behind Jordan's until sundown. The coolness came up from the river across the valley, and the sky was wide and moist and pink-streaked. He remembered the brush-dance. He stretched up, but had to sit back because the beer still bulged in his stomach. He got up later.

The town people came to the brush-dance pit because it was part of the Fourth of July. They were sitting lumped along the sides of the octagonal pit, looking down into its emptiness. They watched, waiting. It was after 8:00. The night came clear and slate-clean. Except for some insects making picking sounds close to the ground, there was an even quiet. The people had wrapped themselves in their oldest jackets against the quiet. When several stars had sharpened through the night sky, Joe Smoker's wife came to start the fire in the center of the pit with the wild celery root. She went down on her knees and blew quick breaths beneath the celery roots until the fire glowed and glowed and grew great in a rush.

The dancers in dungarees came down after her. There were only old men to begin things. Ray Fischer was there and Abraham Hardrock, who had brought the abalone bracelets and the necklaces of smooth pine cone seeds for them to wear and the feathers and the fox-fur quivers. The dancers followed each other around the inside of the pit until they were in a

17

circle with Joe Smoker's wife still sitting in the center. They started slowly with the hollow humming. In a while the humming became, "Hi-i-i-e, hi, hi, hi." It pricked the quiet. The dancers hitched up their feet in time to it. Suddenly on a high hark they stopped and unwound themselves out of the pit. Joe Smoker's wife stayed down in the stillness in the center of the pit. She waited and stroked her sides. The Bureau of Indian Affairs paid her to come and be medicine woman for the Fourth of July, and she had braided bits of fur into her hair. Up above her, around the edges of the pit, the people were commenting on it all. Now and then a face appeared in the darkness when someone lit a cigarette.

In the next dance there were old men and some of the pudgy boys. They had brought beer over behind the pit. Some had on their silky shirts with pineapples printed on them besides having feathers fixed over their ears. Again the dancers went around Joe Smoker's wife, and they were singing the high song until someone from the seats up above said, "Make it short and sweet." Then the singing became low. The dancers began to move themselves around and around the pit. Ray Fischer's eyes slanted shut. He kept lifting his legs up and down. Except for his legs it seemed he was slumbering in his sheep skin.

Some of the boys started in singing, "Shake, rattle, and roll. Shake, rattle, and roll. Joe-Dee-Maj-Joe. Marlan Man-Roe. Joe-Dee-Maj-Joe." The words rolled into the low song, and the pudgy boys laughed loosely. All above them the people laughed along. Ray Fischer saw the lady sitting up above, and he could remember back to a few minutes in the morning. He came out of the circle to say to her, "Ain't it pretty like? Ain't it pretty? Ain't it?"

"We've been looking for you," she said. "I told my friend. It's really-really interesting. But I don't get what all the hopping stuff's for."

18

Ray Fischer said, "Young boys no dance. I dance brush-dance. It's a feet-song. Feet-song." He rubbed the palms of his hands across each other.

"Lovely," said the lady. "Real lovely and interesting. You can teach me how someday!"

Ray Fischer placed his fingers over the edge of the pit. "Show brush-dance now. Show, show," he said.

He stepped through the circle of men to the center of the pit. They had started singing the high song again. Strands of smoke were seeping from the sides of the fire and twisting up together out of the pit. Joe Smoker's wife shifted the fire about with a stick so the wild celery smell streaked up with the smoke. To the four corners Ray Fischer shook his fox-fur quiver. Because of the shine from the fire and the sweat, his skin gleamed seamlessly. Only a pocket of shadow showed under his lower lip. He sang a lone high solo straight up into the stillness of the night. It thinned out in the high silence of the stars. Ray Fischer danced as high as he sang. So high the strength sank out of his legs. He stumbled down in the center of the pit, and Joe Smoker's wife moved aside. The people were clapping. Ray Fischer covered his face with the fox-fur quiver. Over him the others kept humming the hollow song.

BONE

Myrtle Riegle was half-Hoopa and half-Irish—her mother was a full-blooded Hoopa and the Irish came from her father, who came into the valley with Ulysses S. Grant and the American Army. She was astonished by her daughter-in-law who said that, for herself, she was an American and proud of it.

Myrtle Riegle's son had gotten this girl from down around Berkeley when he was there looking for a job. When he couldn't get a job, he came back to the valley with the girl. Two weeks ago she had returned to the city. To take a summer vacation, she said. Now she was back in the valley again. On Monday she came over to see Myrtle Riegle to tell her about the vacation.

Myrtle Riegle lived on the long road that the timber trucks took up out of the valley to the high forests. At the beginning of the road, where it forked from the main route, the soil was coarse with sandstone bits. Some people had set up trailers on this coarse land, but Myrtle Riegle's house was halfway up the road, about where the valley started to disappear into the Siskiyou Mountains. The ground here, back from the main route before it became mountain rock, was sponge-soft and good for growing things. Behind Myrtle Riegle's house were a water spot and a willow, its slips of leaves always slightly stirring. Close around the front and sides of the house was a flat-slatted fence, with all the space inside the fence in flowers and garden. Stems and leaves meshed together in a greenness so dense there seemed to be no solid soil. They tangled through the fence and through each other, some columbine tangling over and around the wires Myrtle Riegle had rigged from fence to house, its tendrils loose and twisting down.

A gate was set in the fence. The daughter-in-law lifted off the ring of rubber tubing latching the gate. It hung heavy on its hinges, and she had to nudge it open, grating it across the ground. At the same time, she was calling, "You-hoo-You-hoo-You-hoo! Where are you, Mother Riegle? Where are you, Mother Riegle?" And then, "Oh, there, I see you on the porch. I'll be right up."

Myrtle Riegle was at home on her porch. "How are you, daughter-in-law?" she asked. Inside the fence, the great greenness surrounded the daughter-in-law. Here the shadows shed from the Siskiyous merged with the sharpness of the sun and formed moisture. With the poppies, jewel lilies, marigolds, and scarlet gilias, the daughter-in-law seemed to glow orange and golden out of the greenness. But only momentarily, before she moved toward the porch.

"Did you bring me a present?" asked Myrtle Riegle.

"I brought myself," said the daughter-in-law. "On this simply sizzling day." She went on, "You know we have air-conditioning in Berkeley. In all the houses."

"Air-conditioning," mused Myrtle Riegle, amazed at this daughter-in-law. She had been in air-conditioning once in the movie-theater in Eureka.

The daughter-in-law sat on the corner of the porch day-bed. She crossed her knees. "Whew! I'd almost forgotten how really bad it can be around here. And since I've been back, there's been nothing to do except be hot. And make sandwiches for Sam's lunch, for him to take up to the woods. Peanut butter and lettuce. Peanut butter and jelly. Peanut butter plain. In Berkeley we had steak once in a while for supper."

Trumpet vines had been trained to twine about the porch posts and to stretch along the rim of the roof. A Japanese wind-chime was tied up from a place under the vine, and when the air moved, the flat pieces of glass made a small shattering sound against each other. Myrtle Riegle was sitting in an over-stuffed brocade chair. With the day-bed and the chair, the porch was crowded. Lying around were years of well-creased movie magazines.

Before her daughter-in-law came over, Myrtle Riegle had felt free in only a slip, all the fine lines of her settling breasts showing. But knowing the daughter-in-law was coming, she had shaken herself into something decent. She wore the pink dress with three little bows on the bodice and, of course, the gold earrings the daughter-in-law had given her for Christmas. It pleased Myrtle Riegle to have these bright ornaments that set off her face. She also had had time to cover over her smatterings of freckles with a pink-white powder.

"You had a good time in Berkeley?" Myrtle Riegle asked. In the garden the heat was steady and shimmering, but on the porch it seemed to shift a little.

"A simply gorgeous time," said the daughter-in-law. "Something doing all the time. And like I said, since I've been back here there's been nothing doing except to be hot. Hot-hot-hot. Nights in Berkeley we would go over to some people's like Betty's and Arty's. I went to school with Betty all the way through the eleventh grade, and anyways we'd go to the movies or something." She stopped. "Hey, you got some new movie mags since I been gone."

"I be liking to read these days," said Myrtle Riegle. She smoothed out the shiny cover of a magazine with a large smiling face on it. "In the magazines you can go for miles away. I never have all that schooling you got. I only have four years, and that when they sent us out to Carlisle School in Pennsylvania. We went on lines of horses, across the rivers until we all got on the train and got to Pennsylvania. Then we came back to the valley after four years." The pieces of glass in the Japanese wind-chime were twirling on their strings.

"School's all right, I guess," said the daughter-in-law. She scratched herself under her arm. "So in the afternoons I used to go shopping downtown. This time of year there were lotsa sales for dresses, but the bathing suits hadn't come on yet. Once when I was down with Betty—she knows about Sam being some Indian and all—she takes me to this museum where there was some Hoopa stuff. White deer skins for a special dance and some old woodpecker heads. And there were some displays-like, showing how to make acorn soup. It was pretty interesting, I guess."

"They got those old things down there?" Myrtle Riegle thought about Abraham Hardrock and Rachel Parker. If they knew about that, they wouldn't like it much. "I ain't got any of those old things. No baskets even. My old mother taught me how to do them, but I just forgot." Myrtle Riegle got up to get some Kool-Aid from inside the house.

"Anyways," the daughter-in-law said, "I got a new dress. It's sort of crinkly." Myrtle Riegle came back to the porch with a pitcher.

"I like a new dress," she said. She poured the sweet purple water out first for the daughter-in-law. The daughter-in-law swallowed it straight down. And then the girl said she had to be going.

After the daughter-in-law left, Myrtle Riegle kept sipping the Kool-Aid. Sometimes she tipped the glass up so that the ice cubes slid down and clinked against her teeth. She was confused about Berkeley and the white deer skins being there. Myrtle Riegle had watched the special dance with the sacred skins suspended from sticks held high in the air. She was listening now, and through the sounds of the wind-chime and the garden insects, she heard the shrill whistling sound that the old men had made on the heron-leg flutes when they danced. The whistling became a worshipping song when the old men would press their obsidian spears against their chests and sigh. A stillness settled into the valley, but Myrtle Riegle could not think of what to do now.

She went into the garden and stood surrounded by its steaminess. She had her shoes off, and her feet were splayed. Specks of sweat began to show out of the powder. Myrtle Riegle never spent time in the garden straightening things because there was always one more place to be planted, and she'd rather do that. She knew now she had some sunflower seeds saved under the porch. She crouched down to see into the dank darkness. Other things she had also stored there. Mostly old things that the house could no longer hold, like picture frames and jars, a shovel, a cradle, besides the sunflower seeds on a shelf. She huddled the seeds in her hand awhile before she decided where they should go in the garden.

Myrtle Riegle spent the rest of the afternoon setting in the sunflower seeds along the fence, every eighth slat. When they were grown, they would nod out over the fence. She dug the holes with a big toe. The wide shade was beginning to spread down from the Siskiyous, and slender shadows were beginning to shoot out from under the leaves in the garden when her son stopped off at the house. He shouted to her while he was screeching the gears of the truck to a halt out in front and the red road dust was still rising up, "Hey, old lady! Guess what!"

The son had always been a sort of joker. He got out of the truck and came to speak to her across the fence. He had a load of logs on the truck, so he couldn't stay long and besides some of the boys who worked in the woods were with him. "Just wait till you see what me and the boys brought you back!"

With the shadows there was a mossy moistness about the garden now. Myrtle Riegle waited by the fence. Against her ankles the garden grasses were slivers of coolness. "Did you bring me a present?" she wanted to know.

One of her son's friends said, "You bet we did. Sam's always saying about you being interested in things."

The other friend brought a big something out of the truck. "Bone from the mountain," he said.

"Mastodon bone," the son said.

"Foreman says they've got plenty of mastodons these days," said the second friend.

Sam explained, "We had the Caterpillar and were shovin' up some stumps. Then there was this thing sitting there. Sort of in this stump. Sitting right there. So I said 'Shucks' and brought it along. Couldn't leave it just sitting there. Didn't do anything just sitting there. I guess there must've been some other bones too."

They came inside the fence and set the bone down on one of the steps to Myrtle Riegle's house. "Keep it polished," the son said. "See you tomorrow at the square dance," he said.

The bone bulked big on the step. It was made bigger by the shadows from the half-day. It was a possession. Its substance was a stippled white, and its sides were outspread wings. Drawn down toward the center of its shape were sharp lines which might have told how old it was. Myrtle Riegle mused on the bone. "Mastodon," she sounded to herself. Made when the mountains were made. Before the old men. And the rest of the mastodon still caught in the stump roots. Massive and unmoving. Myrtle Riegle let the bone with its outspread wings sit by itself on the step. She sat on the step below it.

In the evening on Tuesday, Myrtle Riegle went down to the square dance at the school in the Square where they had the Bureau of Indian Affairs building. Every Tuesday she went down to sit along the sides and see the young people and the Square people and to have someone serve her small cookies on a plate. This Tuesday Myrtle Riegle wore her yellow satiny dress and her silver necklace. She appeared quite proper. Wallace Batter was there finding tunes on his violin. He stood solidly on one foot, with the other one tapping in time to the tunes. Whenever something sounded wrong, he put the bow between his teeth and leaned over the violin to tighten the wires. Opal Flanagan, who played on the accordion, was sitting behind him. These two had some Hoopa blood in them. Then there were the Hickman boys, who had come up from Arkansas to saw sugar pine in the valley. They had steel guitars and had set up microphones and magna-boxes everywhere so the sheer sounds of their guitars would slash through the crowd.

Myrtle Riegle sat by herself in the center of a bench to wait and see. Rachel Parker had come only once to the square dance. She had said to Myrtle Riegle about how she did not like the new kind of songs. More people were coming in. The young girls came in fuchsia skirts with little lockets on slender chains lying on the smooth skin of their chests. The boys in slim black suits were there with their black hair clipped on top into bristles and brushed back long on the sides. And there were the Square people and Hoopas like Hank Henderson, who made sure the logs were sliced right at the sugar pine mill. Myrtle Riegle's son and her daughter-in-law in her new dress came and went around saying hello to everybody. But things didn't get going until Mr. Ralph Gordon of the Bureau of Indian Affairs arrived. He wasn't long in getting there.

He grasped one of the Hickman's microphones in his hand, "Grab your partners. Now's the time. Let's go-go-go. GO everybody!" and soon they were all swing-swing-swinging. The girls' skirts swirled out, and their shoes swung off out over the floor. The little lockets lunged forward. "Dig for the oyster! Duck for the clam!" Opal Flanagan was making wide sweeps with the accordion, and the Hickmans were really stomping the floor. "Promenade-promenade-promenade. Everybody home for some lemonade," called out Mr. Ralph Gordon on the microphone. The clashing colors slowed to a stop, and there was a sweaty pause from the clattering sounds before they all began again. All the time Ray Fischer, the old Indian, was looking through the window from the outside. Sometimes the scrawny dogs, which were always lying around the Square would leap

27

up past him, over the sill, and run in crazy circles around the dancers.

People began to get tired halfway through and came over to sit on the bench by Myrtle Riegle. They passed out the cookies halfway through, too, and Myrtle Riegle made her hands small in her lap. Under the white glare of the school lights, her silver necklace gleamed. By the main door of the school there was a thick yellow light to keep the bugs away, but because of the white light inside, they kept rasping against the screens. Myrtle Riegle's son and daughter-in-law came up to her now.

"Hey, old lady," the son said, "tell them about what we got in the woods yesterday."

"Mrs. Riegle," said someone who lived in the Square, "you must drop in to see us. Not just for the square dance, you know."

"What did Sam give you, Mrs. Riegle?" somebody else asked, and offered a cookie.

Myrtle Riegle smiled because she had the beautiful feeling of knowing that the big bone belonged to her. "He brought me a bone," she told them.

"Really?"

"Mastodon," said Myrtle Riegle.

"Mastodon?" asked someone else.

"Mastodon bone in our woods?" asked Hank Henderson.

"And it's all bone," the son said.

"Whereabouts in the woods? Were there other bones? How many? Why didn't you notify someone? Who was with you?" These were the questions Hank Henderson asked. But Myrtle Riegle just sat smiling in the center of the bench so the son had to do all the explaining.

"The foreman said they've got plenty of mastodons these days."

Myrtle Riegle, no longer feeling alone, said, "It's a big bone he brought me. You must drop in to see it." People moved in to hear what was being said and moved out again.

Mr. Ralph Gordon moved in. "Mastodon bone," he said. "Miz Myrtle's got a mastodon bone, has she? Mastodon bones belong in museums. For the American people."

"The foreman said—" her son began.

"Sam," said Mr. Ralph Gordon, "I don't care what he said. He don't know what he said. But I know anything up in the woods is the property of the American government. I say that bone is property of the American government."

Myrtle Riegle said, "That bone is mine."

"Now," the son said, sidetracking, "I guess we can let that bone go. Just an old bone. Like any old bone. Just brought it back cause it wasn't doing any good sitting there."

The daughter-in-law said, "In Berkeley we put the old steak bones in the garbage every night. Couldn't very well keep them sitting around the house forever. One time I heard about ptomaine coming from having old bones around."

"That's right," said Mr. Ralph Gordon. "Think of it now—" and he stepped outside the circle around the bench where Myrtle Riegle was sitting. He took up the microphone again and tilted it up to him so his voice would blare through the school. "Think of it now—in headlines three inches high. Mastodon bone found here. Here in this valley. I can just imagine. In headlines three inches high." He stopped. "Does everybody here know Miz Myrtle Riegle has got a mastodon bone? A gen-u-ine A-mer-i-can bone!"

Myrtle Riegle understood the questions now. She kept her hands small in her lap, but the specks of sweat started to show through her powder. "She's going to give it to us, and there'll be headlines three inches high," Mr. Ralph Gordon said, and when his voice stopped searing her ears, Myrtle Riegle left the school. They had started in swinging their partners again.

"Birdie-in-the-cage. Circle-circle-three hands 'round!'"

On the long road to the high forest, past the trailers and toward her house, the night lay motionless. The small sounds of insects speckled the silence and then disappeared into it. Myrtle Riegle walked with her shoes off. Bats folded themselves through the stillness, and everything seemed only a shadow of itself.

In the garden the shadows lay undisturbed beneath the leaves of the flowers. But Myrtle Riegle had to disturb this quiet in order to move the bone. It was still on the step with its wings outspread. Myrtle Riegle bent down to wrap her arms around it. As she carried it, its wings protruded over her shoulders. She placed the big bone under the porch with the other still precious things. She would let it stay there. The quiet returned and settled in.

When they came down in the morning from the Square, Myrtle Riegle was sitting in the center of the day-bed on the porch, over the place where the big bone rested with its outspread wings.

THE WHITE-SKIN DEER

The No-Good. The No-Good. Daniel Parker Spotz, the No-Good. She sank the basket again and again into the shallow river current, each time massaging the acorns, loosening their shells, and the words performed an accompanying counter rhythm in her mind. The motions involved in leaching acorns were easy ones for Rachel Parker. Usually in the morning she would poise here on the brink of sleep, softening the acorns into the palms of her hands, and the river would talk its mundane talk to her. A quick action in the shallows: a storm along in the afternoon. A roar in the channel: salmon running. But Rachel Parker was talking to herself this morning: The No-Good. The No-Good. Daniel Parker Spotz, the No-Good.

Last night, he had convinced the old man, Abraham. He shouldn't be thinking of tiring out. She raised the basket. He shouldn't be thinking of tiring out, but of the people, of the kin, of her, too. He knew it would spoil the world forever. He knew they couldn't have the dance until the tenth month, which was when they had it all the years before. To change the ceremony to the eighth month would seem he was thinking more of the white man's calendar. The tenth month had always been the right time, the ripest time. Dried salmon were plentiful from the springtime, and new acorns came in. The river lulled the people to sleep on the sands. Now in the eighth month, the sands kept the heat of the day through the night. They would have to sleep on cinders and firestones. An old man, Abraham. He shouldn't be sleeping on cinders and firestones. An old man, but not so old. A Hoopa.

In another month or two, he might have his singing voice again. A shivering sickness had spread over Abraham and over many of the people when the floods drove down the river this year. Lillian Parker Spotz, come back to visit, had died in their father's hut, leaving her sister the hut with their father's and their father's fathers' treasures and leaving her sister her son, Daniel Parker Spotz. However, Daniel Parker Spotz—the No-Good—did not stay, but moved into one of the Industries' trailers; he wasn't going to belong to her. But Abraham had survived the sickness, and about the time of the first hot winds, Rachel Parker noticed he started telling the dogs to get out of his way again. Soon he was taking Young Rabbit's shoulder to get him to the sweat-house. Rachel Parker had waited many days, stretching her ear toward the sweat-house, expecting each day since the time of the first hot winds to be the day when Abraham would sing.

The acorn shells were loosening; she nudged out a few kernels. And the mist on the river's surface was beginning to stir, shifting its weightless weight, changing to a mass of loose and coiling strands. She remembered the day when Abraham had asked Young Rabbit to take him in the pick-up to Bald Mountain and to come back for him at sundown. Rachel had known what he was going to the spirits' place for, and she had prepared dried salmon for him when he returned. Now, last night when he had told Daniel Parker Spotz that the dance could start anytime, she knew he hadn't found his singing voice on the mountain and didn't care about living or dying.

His singing voice was the voice that the gods had given him when he came from the headwaters of the world. This was the voice that he had given to the people every year at the time of the dance. Twisting and leaping, Abraham's voice, together with the white-skin deer heads, took the people from the geography of their valley and the geography of themselves to their beginnings behind Bald Mountain and together poured them back into the river of sky. So they floated in the world renewed. But Abraham's singing voice seemed to have been snatched into the spring-flood and to have drifted out of the valley.

Most of the kernels were free now; they settled into the bottom of the basket, their husks rising to the surface, easily skimmed off and cast bobbing into the current. Rachel Parker pinched off the last casings. She knew Abraham was not tiring out. It was only the eighth month, and he was walking and talking well. But Daniel Parker Spotz had talked better, last night.

Rachel twitched the last husks out of the basket. The cabled white mist was dissolving although long strands of it were still snagged in the brush on the opposite shore, and the mountains' shadows kept the river dense as obsidian. Seen from the opposite shore, Rachel Parker, as she lifted the basket for the last time, might have appeared to be another animal lifting its head from drinking. But immediately that rack of antlers became a large squat basket, and Rachel became what she was. A heavy woman with a wonderful diligence. She always reached the river before the other women in the valley came to leach their acorns and rose from the shore to start them cooking before the sun had sunk the shadows into the river's depths. She stepped back from the shallows to the edge of hard sand and was patting it with her foot.

The No-Good. The No-Good! She thought. The dance could not be earlier than the tenth month. Earlier would spoil the world. And it depended on her, too. She needed time to get ready. Her fathers had the greatest of the people's dance-treasures, so her fathers' house had always been the host. Decisions were hers now. Lillian had floated back to the beginning on the satin pillow her son had set beneath her head, but the treasures were not to pass to the No-Good. She could argue as her fathers would have argued. Decided, she listened to the river again. A steady droning in the central channel was the sound of a thousand bees swarming downstream, almost certainly a usual eighth-month day.

But wait. On the opposite shore, where the strands of mist were unwinding from the brush, Rachel Parker saw the ghost of a form. Above the sound of the running river was suspended a vision of a white-skin deer. The head, a perfect lily, turned upon a slender stalk-like neck to gaze at the woman. Quick-eyed herself, she caught the glance of the deer's quicker red eye, a bright spangle against the snow-white skin. The look that the deer gave across the water was steady, unhurried. The look Rachel Parker gave in return wavered and fell to the river. Sunlight slid down the mountains and out over the river, and Rachel Parker looked again. "O White-skin Deer. O Fathers. You do not blink." The deer flicked a perfect petal of an ear. The sun touched a shoulder, and a shudder rippled and sparkled over the opalescent flank. "We will wait until the tenth month to hear you sing." Shadows and mists gone, the deer stepped out into the sun to the river's edge and drank. In full view—not large, but leaning toward the water like a drawn bow stretched in the spring from a birch sapling. Even as it raised its head, there was no release of tension, only the sure gesture of beauty. The red eye stared beyond Rachel Parker, and when she turned to follow its course, the deer swerved. She saw it shimmer and vanish in the underbrush. But not before it soundlessly snapped a translucent hoof. She stood enclosed in the silence of her vision until the droning of the bees overcame her again, and she felt her fingers gripping the sides of the basket of newly leached acorns.

Daniel Parker Spotz, a young man, sat in a chair on his Aunt Rachel's porch this morning and waited for her return. They called him "The No-Good, The No-Good," but he had a plan. Always in October, the things which gave all the people meaning were brought out for the dance from his aunt's, his mother's, and his grandfather's hut—the cool and shining obsidian blades, the bands of sea-lion teeth, the strings of money-shells, the condor feather headdresses, the skirts of civet-cat fur, the quivers of otter skin. He ticked off the items, concluding with the deer skins, remembering their eyes of bright red woodpecker heads, their soft tongues of embroidered buckskins, their ears stiff with fine red feathers and still alert. And although the quivers had seemed more worn and the deer skins were becoming a murky blue, as Daniel had watched them carefully folded and unfolded each year during his boyhood, he had longed to embrace them: to hold a blade and raise it to pierce the roof, to take up a deer head and to become the strange beautiful creature which, during the dance, could leap through the smoke on the path cut by the obsidian blades to the sky. All the people had these dreams, but they no longer disturbed him since he had gone with his mother to the city.

Daniel Parker Spotz tilted his chair back and looked toward the river, his eye tracing the path his aunt had taken across the rough gravel to the point where she would have dropped down the embankment to the water's edge. The focus of his gaze became lost then in the mist, but he let his mind wander downstream to the Rutherford Trinity River Lumber Industries. He saw in his mind's eye the tall conical form of the sawdust incinerator rising up solid out of the mist. Surrounding the incinerator was the rest of the operation: the office, the sawmill, the lumberyards, the docks, and his own trailer off to the south with those of other Industries men. Daniel Parker Spotz fancied himself astride the incinerator for a moment to watch the activity. Trucks came in from Bald Mountain unloading logs. Logs spilled down the river, were snatched up at the docks, and swung into piles. Logs were fed into the mill, trimmed, planed, diminished, and changed to lumber. The lumber was stacked with precision in the yards. Daniel watched himself scurry with the rest. All day long he hooked the great logs off the piles and flipped them onto the conveyor belt, which took them into the saws, stepping each time out of the way as if he continued the reel-dance he had learned in the white missionary school. These weirdly animated logs were his perpetually changing partners. The whistle down at the Industries blew, and Daniel continued to sit atop the incinerator in his imagination, watching himself hustle to get in line at the paymaster's window in the office building. There were two things he could do with the forty dollars he collected every two weeks: spend it on whiskey in Willow Creek or sink it in stock in the Rutherford Trinity River Lumber Industries. He was sinking it in stock, and, sitting atop the incinerator, he saw himself sitting inside the office, behind the paymaster's window where the grizzled white man sat who possessed the trees, the river, and the people.

This was Walter Rutherford, and Walter Rutherford had made an offer to Daniel Parker Spotz. Change the date of the white deer skin dance so that his associates could come up from the university to photograph and study it, to help put the valley and the Industries on the map, and Daniel might come into the office to learn bookkeeping. He knew where Daniel's paychecks were going and was glad he took an interest in the advancement of the Industries. He also thought that with his mother recently passed away, Daniel might have some regalia to sell, perhaps an odd deer skin. His friends were buying such things for museums, giving Daniel a chance for more cash to sink into stock.

Old Abraham had agreed last night, but only because he was tired and didn't think he'd be around to look after things in October. Old Abraham thought of the people, and Aunt Rachel kept insisting that Daniel should think of the people. Well, he figured she would be thinking of the people if she held up the things to these white men, if she let them touch the sliver-sharp edge of an obsidian blade, if she invited them to photograph the deer heads thrust skyward beneath Bald Mountain, and if she sold a quiver to them for eternal preservation in the Sacramento State Museum. If she knew the people could repossess the world with the white man's money. His father, that lumberman turned used-car salesman, must have taught him something.

Rachel Parker came walking back across the rough gravel, the old familiar way, with the old steadiness, her bulk floating on an irreversible current, the movement of her feet imperceptible, the basket jutting from her hip like an outrigger. Her eyes, however, were not fastened on the hut and on the immediate future. They did not pause to observe the young man tilted in a chair against the front of her hut. Rachel Parker was wondering who else had seen the white-skin deer this morning. Remembering the quick shimmer and the translucent hoof, she did not doubt the vision was her own. The memory glittered in her mind and crystallized as she looked at the insolent rake of Daniel Parker Spotz in the chair on her porch. Her unique vision. Not even Abraham's. So the dance would be in the tenth month.

She put the big basket down by the cooking place and scraped the ashes back for the firestones, again involved in the daily ceremonies of her life. She had dry branches ready to place over the stones. She stopped. "Daniel Parker Spotz, I need a fire." She heard the chair tip back down and the hard boots scrape on the slate.

"Auntie, let the fire wait. Let the mush wait. Let me talk now. I'll be going to work soon."

Rachel set the round stones together and balanced the branches over them; she examined the mass of leached acorns. They had gathered good acorns last year and plenty; there was enough here to make a good mush for several days and to provide for Abraham. The first match set the twigs crackling with spurts of flame down to the branches. It would be some time, though, before the heat would penetrate the heart of the stones; she would first sweep the threshold.

"Okay," he said. "The fire lights. You can make a good fire. You can make a good dance."

"The dance is good," Rachel Parker said, "anyways."

"You make the dance good," Daniel Parker Spotz said. "You keep the people's treasures well. The treasures are respected by white men and Indians. The white men want to know the treasures. Abraham Hardrock would agree."

"The treasures will wait until the tenth month," Rachel Parker said. She poled one of the firestones with a stout charred staff. Flakes of flame fell on the stones.

The young man stretched his legs out before him. "And who will dance? Our men can't get time off from the Industries in October. You know. The last logs come then, before the snows."

"The people always come."

"More in the summer. More come then to see the treasures and to eat your mush."

The stones appeared glowing now, and Rachel knocked them against each other with her staff, listening for the brittle clink that signified they could be put among the leached acorns in the basket. With two staffs, she lifted a hot stone into the basket. "Abraham will have new mush," she said.

"That's a good idea. I'll carry the basket over for you," said Daniel.

Rachel Parker had not counted in any way on the next visit of the white-skin deer. Abraham Hardrock lived closer to the road, farther from the river than Rachel Parker; but before the road was worn through the valley by timber trucks, he had simply lived between the river and the mountains. The sweat-house wasn't far from Abraham Hardrock's. The other houses of the people spread out near and far from the sweat-house. James Batter's hut and the Rabbits' were as far away as the bend in the river, but still the sweat-house was the center, and Abraham was the closest to it. The track between his hut and the sweat-house was as clearly traced out through the low grass as the track between Rachel's and Abraham's.

Since dawn the old man had been sitting on his hut's threshold. He had slept too long during the fever-sickness, and now he did not sleep as before; nor was he awake as before. Every day as the familiar phantoms passed around him, feeding him, watering him, and tending him, he waited to wake into the beginning, into the world of shining forms. His knees were drawn to his chest, and his hands capped his knees. A thinner man than he once was, he might have been taken for sticks thrown up on the threshold. His breathing was soft and regular, but there was a sudden sharp intake, like the sound of a woodpecker delivering one strong blow and moving on. As the haze began to shift, to settle into the grass, and to disappear into itself, Abraham Hardrock saw suddenly, clearly the small dark discs of an animal's footprints set in the sheen of the grass, and his eye followed the prints across the grass to the apparition of the white-skin deer. A cloud sharpened to precise earthly proportions, its softness made palpable. The animal dipped its beautiful head to the moist grass, and milk seemed to flow under its hooves from an invisible source. Its new points seemed to be the untouched nipples of a young girl. "O Shining One. The first to come. I waited for you. Now you wait for me. Not long." The deer raised its head and stood motionless, its feet poised together on a single spot, as if bound with unseen threads. It gazed at the old man for an instant; then the threads snapped soundlessly, and the animal sprinted into the haze in the direction of the mountains.

It rose, floated, and as the sun burned off the distant haze, Abraham pursued the course of the deer, following its miraculous ascent into a cloud again. The moon, a white flake in the pale sky, would receive the fleet, flying animal, Abraham knew, and moon and deer would fade together as morning became noon. But the waiting was over, for the moon bearing the deer would return. And the people would dance the deer's dance, and he would sing for the last time. He had already told Daniel Parker Spotz, poor No-Good, that the dance could happen anytime, for without a voice he was not in charge. He had not believed he would sing again.

He felt the shadows of people approaching him, coming up from the river, pressing across the grass. And as the weight of these shadows increased, he focused his attention upon the glowing spot in the sky where the moon and the deer within the moon had faded. They had come so early today: Rachel Parker and Daniel Parker Spotz, the last Parker. Rachel took a place sitting on Abraham's threshold. "I brought hot mush," she said. Daniel Parker Spotz set the basket before the old man, but the hands of the old man did not uncap his knees, and his eyes did not leave the sky as he greeted them, "Thank you."

"We will join you," said Daniel Parker Spotz.

"Welcome," said Abraham.

Rachel dipped two fingers into the heavy liquid mass. "It's still warm," she said. The warmth of the mush settled through her; the bitterness had been soaked out of the acorns, and the mush was as flat and as bland as it should be. Daniel scooped up a portion. In the trailer and usually in a hurry in the morning, he had come to rely upon packaged cereal from the grocery in Willow Creek. As long as his mother had lived, even in the city, he had eaten some kind of mush for breakfast. Its heat, seasoned with the salt of the palms of his hands, had slipped him from sleep into the waking day; he had forgotten in these months alone its necessity. Abraham did not eat; he waited. They would speak, and then they would go. Rachel Parker started, "Old Father. Eat and the people will be able to hear your voice."

Abraham let the words move past him; they had no shape. Until Rachel Parker said, "Old Father, the white-skin deer came to me by the river this morning. It came from our fathers to me. To tell me that we do not need to change the time of the dance. You will be singing in the tenth month."

"The white-skin deer also came to me this morning," said Abraham. "I am to follow it. I will sing over the fire and the roots. I can sing once more." He spoke absolutely.

"Don't worry. Young Rabbit can do the singing. The dance is plenty," said Daniel. The plan was possible. Daniel Parker Spotz welcomed Abraham Hardrock and all the albino deer the old man could muster to join him. But the old man didn't have to kill himself.

Rachel Parker heard again the soundless snapping of the translucent hoof. So the deer had come not to her alone. It had come to restore the song to the people. She'd have to get ready. "When will you be able to sing?" Rachel asked Abraham.

"When the moon returns, when the deer returns," Abraham answered. "In five days."

"I need time for preparations. To get the treasures ready and the food."

"I'll tell Mr. Rutherford to be ready with his white men," said Daniel. "Can I help you any, Aunt Rachel?"

Their words had shape now; they were like the small grey fish in the river's shallows, aimless, and Abraham let them pass around him. They urged him to eat; he did not want to eat; but nevertheless, he ate. Rachel took the basket afterwards into his hut in order to leave some of the mush for him; she told him he had to eat. They left. Rachel took the track back to the river, an old woman balancing the lightened basket with ease on her hip, now, like a young girl. So it was settled.

In the evening, Rachel stopped awhile and listened. She had spent the day taking stock. If the dance were held in the

41

tenth month, there would be no calculations to make; she could use all of the acorns out of the storage baskets, for immediately after the dances they would be gathering them anew; now with the dances early, for Abraham's sake, she had to calculate to save enough for the months before they gathered again. For Abraham's sake. She had bought vegetable roots and grapes in the afternoon from the people living near the sweat-house, and the people by the bend had enough salmon and were setting traps for eel. She had started leaching several baskets of acorns when she came home. Now she sat at the threshold and listened.

The sounds of dusk had several levels: the river's steady progress beneath it all, the crisp sounds of the charcoal changing to ash, the last insects finishing and the night birds beginning, long and low. Above the birds, she heard nothing. The moon conceived itself silently out of the mountains and bulged up into the sky; the first stars made no noise.

Abraham, Abraham. Sing or don't sing. To hear him sing would be to hear him live as well as to hear him die. She heard the small sounds of the valley stretching into the silence of the sky, yet she could not ease herself skyward toward this silence because of the noise in her own mind. Abraham, an old man, but not so old. She, an old woman, yet not as old as he. She was listening, but she did not at first hear the song. She did not hear its initial rise until suddenly she realized that the song had forced spaces into the density of the sounds within her mind. She soared with it. Abraham, Abraham. He lived, and his life was precious to them.

Daniel Parker Spotz had done well during the day. Everything had clicked like machinery; Walter Rutherford was pleased: he had made some telephone calls and said, "Okay." Daniel worked overtime to compensate for the lost time in the morning and walked back to Rachel Parker's, stopping at the people's houses along the way to tell them the dance would begin in five days, that Abraham Hardrock would sing. Most already knew because his Aunt Rachel had been by, getting the food going. The moon was livid when he turned toward her hut; he knew her early-to-bed-and-early-to-rise habits, but he knew she would be awake tonight. "All set to go," he announced to her. "I'll get the things out."

"No," she said, and pushing her bulk up against the inside of the doorway, she stood and blocked his way.

"I'll come earlier tomorrow, then," he said. She could not handle all the things. "And Young Rabbit and Ray Fischer and I will carry them when it is time." Only her back refused him as she went inside in response to him this time, and Daniel Parker Spotz, having eaten only a Baby Ruth bar since the acorn mush in the morning, motioned good-bye to his aunt's back and headed for the trailer. He could eat a bear.

In the evenings remaining before they were ready for the dance, Rachel Parker listened for Abraham, and Daniel Parker Spotz went about his business, which eventually, on the morning designated by Abraham for the white-skin deer dance, included loading the things and all the men who would be dancing and Abraham into Young Rabbit's pick-up and taking them up to the dance grounds on Bald Mountain. Mr. Rutherford had given the Hoopa men this day off at the Industries, but some of them had chosen to do overtime and would come on their own in the evening. Rachel did not go up with the treasures because the food was not ready yet; each year she had to trust Abraham to watch to see that Daniel Parker Spotz and the others respected the things as treasures.

When Rachel arrived at the dance grounds, she saw that the men had laid the treasures out carefully. She went immediately to look at them in the madrone grove where the dancers would be dressing later. Young Rabbit's family had treasures, too, and the Fischers and the Batters, and these were also laid out. Rachel looked first at the deer heads, the skins in her family's possession bluing with age, whereas those of the others had gone yellow; she had seen none of them since they had been put away last year, but seeing them, she remembered the bright-eyed deer by the river that no one had seen except herself and Abraham. The heads, propped up on staffs against the twisted trunks of the madrone trees, seemed stiff, their tongues dangling lifeless; the stitching of the red woodpecker feathers bordering the tongues and the ears was perfectly invisible, yet Rachel, with the memory of another shimmering deer, was aware of the stitches.

The blades of obsidian, the cool black stone formed in the great heat of the mountain's creation which the old people had found jutting from the mountain's secret crevices and had chipped to fin-sharp edges, were arranged on buckskin according to length and value. The great ones were as long as a man's arm, but their power came when they were raised, glinting, to parry with the firelight. As they lay motionless, Rachel Parker remembered the deer's clear hooves. And Daniel Parker Spotz. The No-Good. The No-Good. Who could not claim these treasures so long as she lived. She was an old woman, but not so old.

Abraham sat apart in the grove. He had rubbed himself as always for the dance with marrow and soot. Here Rachel could not tend him. For her to see him now would spoil the world. Sight was allowed to only the men and a young girl who was yet clean as spring water. He sat, like the deer heads, with his back propped up against a madrone and ate sparingly what Marjorie Treehouse, the young girl, brought him. His body was a charred remainder. His eyes, however, in his blackened face, glinted like obsidian chips newly brought to light.

Rachel returned to set the food out. The dance ground lay near the base of Bald Mountain, on a stretch of raised land, so the valley could be seen wedged between the mountains, the river its backbone. Below this raised land, the river, where the men had swum themselves clean in the morning, was deep, and the sands, where the people would sleep at night, were wide. Rachel Parker glanced toward the valley as she moved from the place for dance preparations to the place for food preparations. She saw the hot winds, not yet in the mountains, already wavering in the valley. Her glance followed the coiling river to the only projecting point: the conical sawdust incinerator.

She turned to observe that the tables which Daniel Parker Spotz had been carrying in the back of the pick-up had been set up for the food. They had also been covered with green and white cloths. The food—more food than she had seen before at a dance—was stacked on platters; even the salmon that the women had packed away in bark was out. The full round baskets, containing her mush, appeared like unruly muskrats among the elegant abundance of Mr. Rutherford's contributions. Tables and cloths and platters. They had never used these things before. But Rachel saw that the baskets dominated the outlay, and she was confident of the mush. Daniel Parker Spotz, that No-Good, was talking to the white men and bringing them over to the women. Some children were scrambling underneath the tables, seeking shadows; they had their own ways. Rachel Parker joined the women.

"How do you do? How do you do? How do you do?" Mr. Rutherford went from woman to woman, his hand out in greeting. They stood—short, stocky women in ankle-length garments, some distinguishing themselves with headbands patterned with quills and feathers. Some took Mr. Rutherford's hand limply. "You're going to put on a real show for us," he predicted.

"For the people," said Rachel Parker.

"My aunt," said Daniel Parker Spotz.

Mr. Rutherford put forward a hand, and quickly converted a grasp of air into a mere gesture of salutation. "My friend

Daniel says we owe it all to you. We"—he gestured left and right—"Mr. Blessington and Mr. Smith from the University of California."

"There is food to eat," said Rachel Parker. "Come." She had only to wait now for Abraham to sing.

"Eat. Eat," said Mr. Rutherford. "Yes, we've got food here to turn this into a real picnic. Talk can come later." Daniel Parker Spotz, however, intended to talk to Abraham Hardrock now. Mr. Rutherford had let him know that Mr. Blessington wanted a white-skin deer head for the Sacramento State Museum.

The heat, which had collected and hovered in the valley, was beginning to rise. The men had finished dressing for the dance, but Abraham was still sitting beneath the madrone when Daniel passed among the men to come to him. "Old Father, when will we start the dancing?" he asked.

"The fire has been built, but I am waiting," answered Abraham.

"Can the white man speak to you?" Abraham shrugged either yes or no, and Daniel returned with a mandate to the white men. He saw the shining obsidian, still arranged on the buckskins and motionless, as he went back among the men dressed in their tall feathers with the money-shells heavy around their necks, and he saw the deer heads standing against the trees. He thought of stopping to run a finger down the slender ridge of a deer's nose, but he could not stop.

"Daniel, Daniel," said one of the men, "Take a blade."

"Afraid to break a blade?" another asked.

"Take a drink," said another, who had a flask dangling close beneath his skirt. Daniel continued walking, nodding, smiling.

Young Rabbit had started the singing, and someone was blowing shrill whistles in syncopation with the song when he returned to the dance grounds. "The whistles used to be made from herons' legs," Daniel explained to Mr. Blessington.

The dancers appeared now in two columns from the madrone grove, the first pair holding aloft long gleaming blades, those following holding the deer heads high on their staffs. Daniel Parker Spotz continued to explain as the two columns interwove, as the deer heads assaulted each other, and the gods quarreled. It was the beginning of everything. The dust rose, dissolving the feet of the dancers, but the blades and the heads pitched high above the dust. The people, standing all around the dance ground, lost sight of the men as they followed the harsh cadence of the song and the animated deer heads with their flickering tongues and their darting ears. When the dancers slowed to a halt, the heat seemed to sustain their motion, quivering over them all, warping even the sky. Two of the men went immediately to the place where the women sat; they wanted their shoes.

Rachel Parker heard them; they wanted their shoes to dance on the heated sand, these men who had to wear shoes all day long; others would soon want to sit when they watched the dances on chairs the white men had brought; they would want to eat and to chew. "No shoes. No shoes," she said to the men. Shoes and eating and sitting and chewing on the dance ground could work to spoil the world. But they only replied, "Auntie, are you the one who is dancing?" Abraham, Abraham. She wondered if his singing could renew the world this time. She knew Daniel Parker Spotz had taken the white men to see him earlier in the day. Abraham, however, at least knew who possessed the treasures; he would give them no satisfaction.

And he didn't. When Daniel took the white men to him during the long hot afternoon, he had wanted to shake the old man. No pride. Mr. Blessington had a notebook of questions for him, and Mr. Rutherford had offers ready. Daniel had promised to deliver, but Abraham wouldn't deliver; he wouldn't talk. Only Mr. Smith got satisfaction; he took pictures

47

of the old man propped up lifeless against a madrone tree.

There was continued dancing until dusk when the people stopped to eat solidly. Above the people's talking and the white man's questioning, Rachel heard the usual levels of sound. Serving this one and that one mush, she waited, as she had yesterday and days before, for Abraham's song to raise her above these levels. She did not see him take his seat at the dance ground in the place close to the mountain and its spirits, in the place from which the river valley appeared before him. It was the place of his fathers, his fathers who were born of the gods into the valley. Who hadn't heard of the quarrel among the gods and could, like Young Rabbit, recite the events? But only Abraham, who had been at the headwaters of the world, knew how harmony had come from the quarrel, how the valley had been conceived, how the river became the umbilical cord which connected the valley to the floating world of water beyond and remained unsevered.

Abraham's voice, repeating the incantations, began at the level of the coals. Some other people besides Rachel heard it and reassembled at the dance ground. The dancers returned as before in two columns, but the dancers now dipped and swayed the deer heads. They were swimming through waves to merge with the shore, and as before Daniel Parker Spotz was explaining. He knew it all so well, and he knew that his words were trampling the twisting and leaping heart that Abraham's song raised in him.

Mr. Smith's flashbulbs popped, and Mr. Blessington asked questions about the dance ground, the singers and the songs, the dancers and the dance. He held up a little tuning fork to get the pitch, and he squatted down to watch the dancers' feet in order to describe the exact pattern behind the rhythms. Daniel Parker Spotz offered to demonstrate the steps he knew so well. Two-two-three. And Mr. Blessington would certainly like to purchase one of those deer heads. Daniel promised again to provide one. Yes, with the collection just beginning to grow, these splendid examples of Northwest Indian culture were essential, and the museum would pay well. Mr. Rutherford emphasized this last point. Daniel could convince Rachel after the dance was over if they could wait. Perhaps.

Rachel Parker stood at one end of the gathering, Daniel and the white men at the other end. The people flowed in between. From her place, Rachel could keep an eye on the remaining food and on Abraham. She could not see The No-Good. The dust had been laid by the moist shadows which were emerging with the twilight. The dancers swayed in a widening circle, and Abraham's song opened to hold a new world of song. Before him, the fire, which the young girl kept at burning coals, sent out some skeins of smoke and the smell of celery root.

Through these skeins, Abraham saw the pulsating moon, close over the people, close over the valley. He was a man blackened and greased with soot and marrow as he had been blackened and greased so many times before. He could not swallow the moon with his song, for the moon drew him up in long and gradual breaths, and he became singing water. The moon opened and closed its petals, revealing its shimmering, fragrant heart, and Abraham became a sighing stamen at its center. The moon rolled up the mountains of sky, turning to the glistening cave, which would receive the white-skin deer. The people, facing Abraham and the spirit-burdened darkness of Bald Mountain, could see the moon only through Abraham's eyes, but they could see what he could only feel: the milky-white phantom form that appeared behind him.

Rachel Parker saw the white-skin deer, out of the pattern, not swaying in ritual columns, but looking on. Its eyes were dark with the darkness of the mountain behind. Rachel did not understand why the deer had come now. Was it here from the spirits in Bald Mountain to warn or to bless or to consult with

Abraham? While she looked to see if the others were looking, Daniel Parker Spotz excused himself and went to get Mr. Rutherford's rifle from its rack in the back of the sedan.

The gunshot surprised even Walter Rutherford, and Mr. Blessington was irate, for the dancers scattered, and the dance ground overflowed with a mass of people. Daniel had not intended to spoil the dance, but the deer had moved more quickly than he had anticipated and toward the center of the dance ground. He was a good shot and had hit the animal neatly in the throat. "The wound won't matter," he told Mr. Blessington rapidly. "When they fix the skin, they can stitch it up. You've got your skin."

The people watched Daniel and the white men bind the translucent hooves together and drape the deer's pallid form across the automobile fender, its dark red eyes visible wounds.

Only a few slept on the hot sands that night; others left in their own cars or in Young Rabbit's pick-up. But Rachel Parker, an old woman, tended Abraham Hardrock until he died with the moon in the morning.

Two days later, Daniel Parker Spotz took off from the Rutherford Trinity River Lumber Industries to return to Bald Mountain. At Willow Creek, they had tried to book him for hunting out of season and without a license. But Mr. Rutherford, who would have gone bail anyway, reminded the Law that Daniel was Hoopa and didn't need a license to hunt on his own reservation. He needed Daniel to get someone to prepare that skin. But Daniel said he first had to pack the scattered treasures of his fathers for another year and see Abraham Hardrock buried by the river beneath the mountain, his head in the downstream direction. That No-Good. That No-Good.

Hoopa Valley

Portfolio

1956

Ellen Quinby and Elizabeth Schultz, 1956
Courtesy of Anne Alexander.

Hoopa Valley Square Dance, 1956

Hoopa Valley Square Dance, 1956

Lumbering in Hoopa Valley, 1956
Courtesy of Anne Alexander

Bridge over the Trinity River, Hoopa Valley, 1956
Courtesy of Anne Alexander

Swimming in Campbell Creek, Hoopa Valley, 1956
Courtesy of Anne Alexander

BIOGRAPHY

Since retiring from the English Department at the University of Kansas as Chancellor's Club Distinguished Professor, Elizabeth Schultz continues to write academic articles about Herman Melville, essays about the environment, and poetry. In addition to numerous scholarly essays and poems, she has published *"Unpainted to the Last": Moby-Dick in Twentieth-Century American Art*; a memoir, *Shoreline: Seasons at the Lake*; a collection of co-edited essays, *Melville and Women*; the essays for *The Nature of Kansas Lands*; and two collections of poems, *Conversations* and *Her Voice*. She also writes a regular column, "Senses of Place," for the Kansas Land Trust newsletter. Recently, she was a Distinguished Fulbright Lecturer at the Beijing Foreign Studies University and co-organized an international conference in ecocriticism in Beijing.

Mammoth Publications Books

Barnes, Barry *We Sleep In a Burning House: Poems* $10

Day, Robert *We Should Have Come by Water: Poems* $15

Dotson, Carrie *To Francis: Memories of 1930s Kansas* $5

Lassman, Kenneth *Wild Douglas County* $25

Low, Denise & Tom Weso *Langston Hughes in Lawrence: Photos & Biography* $15 paper, $25 hardcover

Low, Denise *New & Selected Poems* (rpt., 2nd ed.) $10

Milk, Theresa *Haskell Institute: 19th Century Stories* $20

Mirriam-Goldberg, Caryn *Learning the Body* $5

Two-Rivers, E. Donald *Fat Cats, Powwows: Poems* $10

Order Online:
www.mammothpublications.com (Pay Pal)

Mail Order:
Mammoth Publications
1916 Stratford Rd.
Lawrence, KS 66044